BABAR'S CASTLE

Written and Illustrated by
Laurent de Brunhoff

Translated from the French by Merle Haas
Random House – New York

© 1962, by Random House, Inc. All rights reserved
under International and Pan-American Copyright Conventions.
Published in New York by Random House, Inc., and simultaneously
in Toronto, Canada, by Random House of Canada, Limited.

Translated from the French. ©1961, by Librairie Hachette.
Publié par les Editions Graphiques Internationales (E.G. I) Paris

Library of Congress Catalogue Card Number: 62-8994
Manufactured in the United States of America

CIP data may be found at the end of the book.

This year King Babar is going to live in
Castle Bonnetrompe. He and Queen Celeste
supervise the loading of all their furniture
and baggage into the moving vans. Then he gives
the signal for departure: "Is everyone ready?"
"Yes!" Arthur, Zephir, the Old Lady, and the
three little elephants answer in chorus.

The weather is perfect as they arrive at
Bonnetrompe. The car climbs the hill leading to
the castle. One can already see the old towers.

The first moving van, too wide to pass through the main gateway into the courtyard, has pulled off the road and parked just outside.

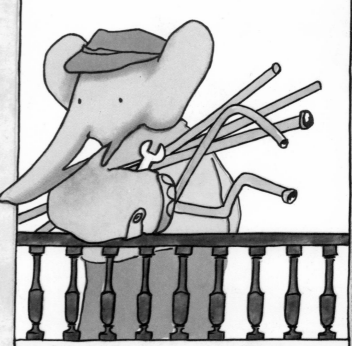

In the impressive
entrance hall, the children
stop to admire the portraits
of their ancestors. "Oh, what
a handsome musketeer!"
exclaims Arthur.
"I like the Roman soldier
better," says Zephir.
As for Babar, he catches
sight of the plumber
carrying his pipes and tools,
and sighs: "Oh, what a nuisance!
The workmen have not yet
finished their jobs."

Because the painter has so much to do, Arthur offers to hang the wallpaper in his own room. While Pom puts a final coat of paint on the door, Flora spreads the paste on the wallpaper. Zephir, standing on the ladder, holds the paper in place against the wall and Arthur presses it on with his trunk. It's not an easy job... Pom has now put aside his paint brushes and is trying, poor fellow, to make some plaster for the ceiling.

And here comes Alexander, black as a coal miner! "Where have you been?" asks Zephir. "In the cellar, trying to find the underground passage." "What do you mean, the underground passage?" "Just that! There's always one in every castle." Celeste, who has come in to see what the children have been up to, is not a bit pleased. "Oh! What a mess! Go take a shower, every one of you, and scrub yourselves with a brush. The bathroom is all finished and ready to be used."

In the big dining hall, the empty suitcases and
trunks are piled high in one corner. The Old Lady is
serving the soup. "Oh goody! Water-cress soup!"
says Arthur. "I love that." "Me too!" says Flora.

Meanwhile, Pom has fallen asleep in a small
trunk. "Oh, the poor little thing," says the Old Lady.
"He worked too hard this afternoon.
Go wake him up gently, Zephir."

In the middle of the night, Alexander gets up and wakes Pom and Flora. "Sh-h-h---Come on! We'll look for the underground passage." In the next room, Arthur and Zephir also jump out of bed. Together they prowl about the castle and find themselves on the roof of the old tower, where an owl has made his home.

Unfortunately the owl has never heard of any underground passage. But he suggests they should go to see the hall of armor, and shows them the way. "Armor and weapons from the Middle Ages!" exclaims Arthur, when he finally finds the switch and turns on the light. "Just like the pictures in my history book at school." With the help of Flora, Alexander and Zephir, Arthur tries on a marvelous gilded suit of armor.

Pom puts on a small black suit and the battle
begins. What a racket! The swords clang
against the steel breastplates. The armor is very heavy
and the two fighters are soon tired and out of breath.
Finally Arthur loses his balance and falls over backwards,
and everyone bursts out laughing... But the noise of his
tumble resounds through the corridors. BANG, BANG, BANG!
The children are scared and run off.

Arthur and Pom had taken off their armor.

But Pom didn't have time to take off his boots.

Back in his room he is in tears because

one of them just won't come off.

5

Zephir
tries to help him...

6

He tugs and tugs; the spur
comes off in his hand!

7

So Pom gets into bed
with his boot on.

8

The next morning
Babar saws it off.

The whole family is now in the great park. With Pom's help, Flora has caught a goldfish in the pond. "I'll keep it in a bowl on my mantelpiece," she says in great glee.

Babar, seated on a brand-new lawnmower, cuts the grass. Arthur rakes up the cuttings and Zephir, as usual, is up to mischief!

Alexander, the inquisitive one, has gone off
for a walk and discovers a little building at the
entrance to the woods. Hearing him call,
the others hurry quickly to join him.
"How beautiful," says Flora, as she runs to the
doorway. "It's so peaceful," says Arthur.
"How about setting up our club here?"
"First let's see what there is inside," cautions Zephir.

They have succeeded in opening the heavy door
and step into a dark room... a library
full of dusty books. Alexander, up on the ladder,
rummages here and there, touching each
of the little sculptured elephant heads
on the top of the bookshelves.
Suddenly a door in the wall pops open.
"The underground passage!" exclaims Pom.

Having found some candles, they cautiously advance in single file. Then they come to a trap door.

A bit worried, they push it up...and find themselves in the living room of the castle! Babar and Celeste are amazed to see Alexander suddenly appearing out of the fireplace. "What is the meaning of this?" shouts Babar. Then he understands. —"Oh, you must have found the underground passage! Good for you, children! Bravo, Alexander!"

A few days later, car after car rolls slowly into
the courtyard of the castle and is parked against
the wall.
Guests of the King and Queen
have come to the
housewarming party.

Babar and Celeste, in their royal robes, greet them on the steps of the grand staircase. Here come Professor and Mrs. Fandago, then Mrs. Hatchibombotar and her children; Mr. and Mrs. Pilophage, and many, many others...

In the ballroom all is joyous and gay. The children,
in great excitement, gather around the buffet table.
Zephir grabs a cherry tart, Arthur reaches out
with his trunk toward the chocolate eclairs.

The Old Lady seated at the piano and the orchestra's
trumpet player invite everyone to join in the chorus.
They all sing the Song of the Elephants: "Patali di Rapata,
Cromda, Cromda, Ripalo, Pata Pata Kokoko."

-29-

Now the children have gone up to bed, but
the party continues merrily until dawn.
Under the pale starlit sky, the
lights of the castle shine through
the windows all night long.
And in their sleep, Pom, Flora, Alexander,
Arthur and Zephir can still hear
the sound of the music floating up
from the ballroom below.

This title was originally catalogued by the Library of Congress
as follows:
De Brunhoff, Laurent Babar's castle; illus.by the author
trans. from the French by Merle Haas. Random House © 1962
30p col illus 1 Picture books for children 2 Elephants—Stories
I Title E, Fic ISBN 0-394-80586-0 0-394-90586-5 (lib.bdg.)

Moving from one house to another is a big event in anyone's life, but few families run into the kind of exciting adventures that befall King Babar, Queen Celeste, and their household when they move into Castle Bonnetrompe.

Helping hang wallpaper, searching for an underground passage, trying on armor from long ago, and finally a grand housewarming party — Babar and his family have a memorable time, and so will the reader.